W9-BWG-634

A Penny's Worth
of Character

A Penny's Worth of Character

by Jesse Stuart

Edited by
Jim Wayne Miller
Jerry A. Herndon
James M. Gifford

Illustrated by
Rocky Zornes

The Jesse Stuart Foundation

A PENNY'S WORTH OF CHARACTER

Copyright © 1954 by McGraw-Hill Book Company, Inc.
Copyright © 1982 and 2021 by The Jesse Stuart Foundation
Illustrations copyright © 1988 by Rocky Zornes

All rights reserved. No part of this book may be reproduced or utilized
in any form or by any means, electronic or mechanical, including
photocopying, recording, or by an information storage or retrieval
system, without permission in writing from the publisher.

Library of Congress Cataloging-in-Publication Data

Stuart, Jesse, date
  A penny's worth of character / by Jesse Stuart; edited by Jim
Wayne Miller, Jerry A. Herndon, James M. Gifford; illustrated by Rocky
Zornes.
      p. cm.
  Summary: Shan is dishonest with the storekeeper in his rural
Kentucky community, but he feels better about himself after his mother
forces him to put things right.
      ISBN 0-945084-32-3 : $5.00.   •
  [1. Honesty-Fiction 2. Kentucky-Fiction.] I. Miller, Jim
Wayne. II. Herndon, Jerry A. III. Gifford, James M. IV. Zornes, Rocky,
ill. V. Title.
PZ7 . S937Pe 1993
[Fic]-dc20   92-31438
                                                        CIP
                                                        AC

Published by:
Jesse Stuart Foundation
P.O. Box 669
Ashland, KY 41105
jsfbooks.com
2021

Dedicated to
Kentucky's Teachers

"I am firm in my belief that a teacher lives on ond on through his students. Good teaching is forever and the teacher is immortal."

-Jesse Sluart

Acknowledgements

This reprint of *A Penny's Worth of Character* was made possible by the generous support of these friends of the Jesse Stuart Foundation:

Julie A. Baker
Roy L. & Barbara A. Brown
Millard (Buck) Byrne
Barry N. & Lynn Ann Cohen
Camila Haney
Jerry A. Herndon
Sherry Horsley
Col. Frank H. Meenach
James F. Phillips
Mary Jeanine Provencal
James A. & Patricia Shope

CONTENTS

"Mom, you got some eggs for me to take to Mr. Conley?" . . .

SHAN'S MOTHER CALLS

"Shan, I want you to go to the store for me this morning," his mother said. "I've got a list made out of things I need."

Shan's mother, Millie Shelton, was doing the family wash before the sun got high enough to shine down into the deep green valley. When the sun got high, the day grew warmer and the flowers wilted on their stems. Then it was almost too hot to rub clothes on a washboard over a tub of warm soapy water.

"Mom, you got some eggs for me to take to Mr. Conley?" Shan asked.

"Not this morning," she replied. "Our hens aren't laying too well this time of year. We're not getting more eggs than we need for ourselves."

Shan was disappointed. When he carried eggs to the store, there were always a few pennies left over after he'd traded the eggs for groceries. His mother let him have these extra pennies to buy candy. Shan was always happy if there were as many as three pennies left over. He bought peppermint sticks and gumdrops with these.

Sometimes there was a whole nickel left over and then he bought his favorite chocolate bar. And sometimes—rarely—there was a dime left to buy the chocolate bar and a lemon soda pop, too. He ate the chocolate bar and drank his lemon soda pop at the same time. The two were so good together that when he thought about them he got hungry. He had never tasted anything better in his life than a chocolate bar when he had a cool lemon soda pop to wash it down.

His mother noticed his disappointment. "Shan, there is a pile of empty sacks in the smokehouse," his mother said. "You can trade them for candy. Don't take the one over on the right by itself—it has a hole in the bottom of it. I'll probably be able to use that one for peaches."

"Thanks, Mom. I'll get them."

Shan began to smile as he thought of the candy he would get at Mr. Conley's store.

He ran to the smokehouse and opened the door. He hurried in and found the sacks stacked up neatly on a chair. There were more than he expected. He counted one, two, three, four, five, six, seven, eight—and very slowly he counted the ninth sack. He had hoped there would be ten. Ten large sacks equaled a dime. And with a dime he could get his favorite chocolate bar and lemon soda pop.

Shan stood there thinking. Then he went over and looked at the tenth sack with a hole in it. It sure was too bad this sack had a hole in it.

14

It sure was too bad this sack had a hole in it.

Maybe the hen had laid an egg this morning.

Shan Makes a Decision

He tiptoed to the smokehouse door and looked out to see where his mother was. She was walking across the yard with another basket heaped high with clothes. She was taking them to the clothesline. The clothesline was on the other side of the yard from the smokehouse. He waited until she set the basket down and started pinning up the clothes. Then he put the nine sacks under his arm and started out.

He stopped; then he went back. He picked up the tenth and looked at the hole. "Not really much of a hole," he said to himself. "A pretty useful old sack if you didn't put stuff like sugar or meal into it."

He knew how Mr. Conley took the top sacks from the pile and held them up to the lighted window and looked inside to see if any light came through. But Mr. Conley was old and he might not be seeing too well. And besides, Mr. Conley never looked at all the sacks. He might look at some on the top and some on the bottom of the pile, but he wouldn't hold every one in the pile up to the light.

Suddenly Shan knew the way to fool Mr. Conley. He put a good sack down. This was number ten. Then he laid down number nine and eight. These were good sacks too. Then he put the sack with a hole in it down for number seven. He placed six good sacks on top. This would throw Mr. Conley off either way he looked. If he looked at the sacks from the top or the bottom, it wouldn't matter now.

Shan smiled as he picked up the paper sacks and held them under his arm. His troubles were over. He had found the way to get what he wanted. He could have both the chocolate bar and the lemon soda, and shucks, what did one little old hole amount to? He walked through the door and stepped onto the soft green grass.

"What's kept you so long, Shan?" his mother asked.

"Mom, I've been counting the sacks," he said.

"The basket is on the table on the kitchen porch and I have my list in the bottom of the basket," she told him as she went back to the tub to rub more clothes over the brass washboard. "Hurry, Shan, because there are things on the list I'm needing now. Don't fool along talking to the birds and wading in the creek hunting crawdads and minnows."

"I won't, Mom," he said.

Shan ran to the kitchen porch and got the split white oak basket his mother had made to carry groceries in. He looked to see if the list was there for Mr. Conley. It was in the bottom of the basket where the wind couldn't blow it away.

Old Rags, Shan's black and white hound, walked over and looked up into his face. He whined as if he were trying to speak.

"You can't go with me, Rags," Shan said. "I'm going to the store."

"Hurry now, Shan," his mother said. "Never mind the hound. And don't fool along talking to turtles, terrapins, and young rabbits."

Shan walked around the big log house. He walked past the chimney that was made of many-colored stones which somebody in years gone by had picked up from the fields. Now the morning glories his mother had planted climbed up the chimney. There were many colors of blossoms: blue, white, and purple, and they were shaped like little bells.

Shan stopped to look at the hen's nest hidden under the morning glories in the chimney corner. Maybe the hen had laid an egg this morning. The hen that laid in this nest seldom missed laying an egg every day. But there was no egg this morning. If there had been, he thought, he might have put the egg in his pocket. An egg would bring two cents, and if Mr. Conley found the sack with a hole in it Shan would still be sure to get his chocolate bar and the lemon soda pop. To think of them made his steps grow faster. It's too bad the hen hadn't laid this morning, he thought as he walked around to the front yard.

The morning was beautiful. Shan heard . . . many wild birds . . .

THE WORLD BELONGS TO SHAN

Shan went through the gate toward the valley road and he stopped once to look back when a pewee flew over his head with something in her bill. She had made a nest of mud under the eaves. And there were young birds in that nest, too. Shan had heard them crying for food. Since he'd never been able to climb high enough to see, he'd often wondered how many young birds she had. He knew there were three young birds in the cardinal's nest. Shan loved the birds. He carried bread crumbs from the table and put them on top of the gateposts for the cardinals. But he didn't have time to watch them now for he had to hurry to Mr. Conley's store to get things for his mother and for himself.

The morning was beautiful. Shan heard the songs of many wild birds hidden among the wild crab-apple trees on either side of the valley. He knew that they were singing because they were as happy as he was. When he reached a big sycamore where people often sat to rest in its shade beside the road, he stopped again. There was a red-headed woodpecker holding onto the steep part of a dead branch with his toes while he bored a hole with his long black bill. He made more noise than Shan's father made when he bored a hole into a plank with a brace and bit.

When the woodpecker saw Shan looking up at him, he stopped to look down at Shan. But he didn't stop very long. He went back to boring into the tree again. Then Shan remembered his father telling him that woodpeckers bored into dead trees to find worms. Shan's father had once shown him, when he was cutting stovewood with an ax, the kind of worms the woodpeckers bored into trees to get. They were little white worms with brown heads. The worms could eat their way into the trees too. Shan thought it was strange what animals and birds like to eat. He knew the woodpecker probably liked such things better than chocolate bars and lemon soda pop.

Between Shan's home and Mr. Conley's store there were three big trees where people stopped to rest themselves and their horses. One was the big sycamore where Shan had seen the red-headed woodpecker. The second one was a white oak with a bushy top and long branches that spread like a big green cloud brooding over the earth. Here people walking along the road would meet each other and sit under the green cloud shade to talk. Shan had passed this tree many times with his father and there would be a dozen neighbors sitting in the shade. Their horses and wagons would be nearby.

Below this white oak was a hole of water, clear and

He found a rock and threw it down at the water snake.

blue, with wild phlox growing on the bank just across from the tree. Wild phlox couldn't grow on the side the tree was, for the tree's giant roots grew above the water. The stream had washed the dirt away from these roots. Shan saw something long and brown lying wrapped around one of the roots. He set his basket in the road and put his sacks into it. He found a rock and threw it down at the water snake. His rock hit the root and jarred the snake off into the water. It swam back under the roots of the tree. He's trying to get his breakfast, too, Shan thought. He's waiting there for the minnows to swim out so he can swallow one.

Shan stood there looking at the water and regretting he had missed the snake. He always tried to kill water snakes because they ate the minnows. He liked to throw bread crumbs into the water and watch minnows swim up and swallow them. He knew something else they liked too. On the side of the white oak was a green fly. Shan tiptoed up and put his hand over the fly. He threw it down onto the water. Then he saw the minnows coming from under the bank on the other side of the stream. Their little silver bodies raced through the clear blue water, and the largest one beat the others and swallowed the fly. They were hungry too, and they wanted their breakfast. Shan found some cracker crumbs under the tree. He threw these into the water and caught more green flies until the minnows had had a good breakfast. Then he got his basket and sacks and hurried on. He knew he wasn't going to stop any more because his mother had told him to hurry.

With his big toe he pursued the crawdad to make him swim.

Now the road and the creek came together. The water was very shallow. Here he had liked to ride in the wagon with his father and watch the horses' big feet splash the water. There was a path around the hill for the older people who wore shoes. But Shan liked to wade in the water. He wanted to feel the water flowing over his feet and around his legs. No wonder the minnows like the water, he thought. He knew it would be fun to be a minnow and swim in this clean, blue water. He knew the minnows breathed water and drank air as he breathed air and drank water. He'd like to try their way of life if it weren't for the snakes. There were these awful snakes that would be waiting to swallow him if he were a minnow.

As he waded down the valley stream he was careful not to splash water. He was afraid he'd get his paper sacks wet. If he splashed the sacks Mr. Conley might go over them really close. And if he did, he might find the hole in number seven. Shan saw a flat rock lying in the bottom of the stream on the slate bottom and he pushed it with his toe. A crawdad came from under it. It swam backward, pulling the water with its fan-shaped tail. It had a pair of little pinchers with pink ends and raised these up in the water when it swam. But Shan had caught crawdads with his hands and let them pinch him and they didn't hurt. With his big toe he pursued the crawdad to make him swim. Shan laughed as the crawdad swam backward into the bank. He pushed more rocks lying on the slate as he waded down the valley stream which was also the road. Soon there were as many crawdads swimming backward and crawling on the blue slate bottom as he had seen minnows in the deep hole under the white oak shade. They were going in all directions and now and then a minnow came upstream and hit Shan's bare leg under the water. This was a lot of fun, but he had to be careful not to splash his sacks.

He looked down into the hole and saw something white.

SHAN'S DISCOVERY

At the very spot where the road left the valley stream and got back onto the dirt again, Shan saw a big brown-and-black checkered object with a long black scaly neck and a little bony head. It was resting on a sand bar. He knew better than to put his toe to its mouth. For this was a turtle and it could bite.

He'd heard his father say that when a turtle bit anybody it wouldn't let loose until it thundered or until the sun went down. As yet the sky wasn't very clear; still, it might be days before it thundered again. The sun wasn't shining in the valley yet and so it would be a long time before sunset. He didn't want the turtle to bite him so he wouldn't give it a chance, but he did want to know what it was doing on the sand bar.

He walked over the dry sand that felt warm to his feet after he had waded in the cool water. He stopped a safe distance from the big turtle. The turtle turned its head sidewise and looked up at him with its bright, beady eyes. Shan wondered how it would feel to be able to hide in a shell. There were lots of things he wondered about this world he lived in. Animals and birds had different languages, and he wondered if they could understand each other. And they liked to eat different things and to eat each other. While he stood wondering about these things the turtle started walking slowly across the sand bar.

On the spot where the turtle had been sitting, Shan discovered a small hole in the sand. He looked down into the hole and saw something white. He set his basket and sacks down again. He put his hand down into the hole and fetched up five turtle eggs. He had often wondered where turtles laid their eggs. This was the first turtle's nest he had ever found. And slowly he put the eggs back into the hole in the sand.

He wondered why he had never found a turtle's nest before. Then he guessed that he had scared the old turtle from her nest before she covered her eggs with sand. They were always covered with sand. That's the reason he'd not found turtles' nests. And he knew the sun on the sand warmed and hatched the eggs. Hens sit three weeks on their eggs and keep them warm to hatch young chickens. Not the turtles—they're smart, even if they do have little bony heads, Shan thought, covering the turtle eggs with sand for the old mother turtle he had scared from her nest.

Shan gathered his sacks under his arm and got his basket. He hurried down the valley road that was winding and narrow under the shades of the tall willows and

Shan screamed, too, as he saw the Cooper's hawk . . .

water birches. The road was sandy and soft to his feet. Shan had to hurry. He had seen so many interesting things and he had heard so many interesting sounds that he had stopped too many times. But he knew he wouldn't stop again.

Shan started running to make up for lost time. As he ran, he heard a wild scream. The scream came from a parent quail to warn one of its family that had strayed. The sun was coming down into this part of the valley and the parent quail had seen the shadow of a hawk as he glided down to get the young quail. Shan screamed, too, as he saw the Cooper's hawk ready to pick up the baby quail in his claws. The hawk arose on fluttering wings, for he was frightened by Shan's voice, and the young quail was saved and got back to his parents.

Shan stopped a minute under the big sugar maple. This was the third big tree between his home and the store where neighbors met, rested, and talked. The bark of this tree was scarred. Each spring it was tapped to get the sap to make syrup. This was the biggest tree Shan had ever seen. It shaded more space than any tree he had ever been under. There were initials and dates carved over its body up as high as a tall man could reach. The grass was worn from under its shade. A gray lizard ran up the side of the tree. Shan watched him catch a fly. He was getting his breakfast, too. But Shan didn't have time to watch so many things. He knew he had to hurry.

As he ran again to make up for time he had lost, butterflies rose in small clouds from the touch-me-nots, buttercups, and phlox beside the road. They were pretty, fluttering clouds with all the colors of the rainbow. Shan heard the rain crows singing their mournful notes from the steep slopes above the road. They're begging for rain, Shan thought. He heard the songs of the cardinals, the chirruping of the ground sparrows, the cawing of crows, and once he heard the big *who-who* of a hoot owl that came from the tall timber. He heard the cries of the chicken hawks overhead. He saw a big hawk circling in the bright wind under the blue sky. The hawk was saying, *chickie-chickie-chickie.* Shan watched him circle high in the bright blue morning air. Then another hawk came flying straight from the tall timber and the two hawks flew away together over the high walls of hills on the other side of the valley. They're hunting their breakfast, Shan thought, remembering the lemon soda pop and the chocolate bar. Now he saw Mr. Conley's store and he started running faster. He would soon be there.

Mr. Conley's store . . . was a little one-room building . . .

MR. CONLEY'S STORE

Mr. Conley's store stood where the valley road joined the Sandy River road. It was a little one-room building, painted white, under a grove of sycamore trees. Shan loved this store, and when he saw it he always broke into a run to get there. He was as happy as he had ever been on this August morning when he stepped up the three little steps into the store.

"Good morning, Mr. Conley," he said.

"Good morning, Shan," Mr. Conley greeted him.

Mr. Conley was standing behind the candy counter. Shan walked up and peeped through the glass to see if Mr. Conley had his favorite chocolate bars. They were under the glass all right. Shan counted six of them. He wished he had enough sacks to trade for all six.

"Gee, Mr. Conley, I was afraid you wouldn't have the chocolate bars," Shan said.

"Yes, Shan, those bars are mighty popular," he said. He walked from behind the counter.

Mr. Conley was a little man. He was bent with age.

"Have you brought me some sacks this morning, Shan?" he asked.

"Yes, I have," Shan replied.

"I'm glad you've brought them," he told Shan. "I need them now. I'm nearly out of large paper sacks. Customers buy flour and meal in small lots and I've used all my sacks."

"I'm glad you want 'em, Mr. Conley," Shan said.

But Shan's heart pounded a little faster when Mr. Conley took the sacks from under Shan's arm.

"Got any holes in 'em?" Mr. Conley asked.

"You . . . y-y-y'd better see for yourself, Mr. Conley," Shan stuttered.

"I always examine them to see if there are any holes," Mr. Conley said.

Shan felt the blood rush to his face. And his heart pounded faster than it did when he was running down the valley. Mr. Conley laid the paper sacks upon the counter. He took the first one and held it toward the window. He opened the sack and looked inside.

"That sack's all right," Mr. Conley said. "When I hold one up against the light in the window and look in, if there's a hole big as a pinpoint it will show big as a dime."

Shan didn't say anything. He couldn't think of anything to say. Even if he could have thought of anything, he couldn't have said it. His tongue felt as if it had been tied down with a twine string—the kind Mr. Conley used to wrap packages. Shan stood there silently as Mr. Con-

36

"Have you brought me some sacks this morning, Shan?" . . .

He took the first one and held it toward the window.

ley lifted up sacks two, three, four, and looked in.

"These are all right, Shan," he said. "I've not found a hole big as a pinpoint."

Then Mr. Conley picked up sack number five.

Surely he won't look at any more, Shan thought.

"This one is all right," Mr. Conley said as he laid it over with the other good ones.

Shan stood there hoping he wouldn't pick up another sack. But he watched Mr. Conley's small nervous white hand as it went down to pick up the sixth sack. Shan felt a warmer glow come over his face. And his heart pounded faster than ever while he watched Mr. Conley open the sack and look in.

"This one's all right," he said and put that sack with the other good ones.

When Mr. Conley reached for the seventh sack, a box of cereal fell from the shelf.

"What was that?" Mr. Conley asked, turning to Shan.

"A box fell off the shelf," Shan murmured.

"I thought somebody had come in the store," Mr. Conley said as he turned back to the sacks. "But when a man gets seventy years old his ears are not as good as they have once been. They get like an old paper sack that has been used so many times it's got holes in it!"

Shan looked up from the floor just in time to see Mr. Conley's little nervous hand go down for another sack.

Oh, I hope and pray he doesn't get that seventh sack, thought Shan.

Shan got his breath easier and his heart slowed down a bit when Mr. Conley took the last sack from the bottom. He lifted it up and looked in.

Sweat ran in little streams down Shan's face now. Mr. Conley reached down and picked up sack number nine. There were only two sacks left. He held number nine and looked at it in a hurry. His hand went down again and rested on the eighth sack. That just left the sack with the hole in it.

"Shan, how many sacks did you bring?" he asked, turning around slowly and looking at Shan.

"T-t-ten, Mr. C-C-Conley," Shan stammered.

Mr. Conley counted slowly. "One, two, three, four, five." This was one pile. "Six, seven, eight, nine, ten."

Shan felt a great relief. Then Mr. Conley picked up the second pile and placed it on top of the first one. Shan knew that meant Mr. Conley would have just one good sack to use before he came to the bad one.

"I'll bet I know what you want for these sacks." Mr. Conley teased Shan as he walked toward the candy case. "You want chocolate bars."

"One chocolate bar, Mr. Conley," he said. "And I want a lemon soda pop."

"All right, my boy," Mr. Conley said, taking slow steps to the candy case. "You'll have the lemon soda pop and the chocolate bar."

Shan's hand was still sticky where he had wiped his face. And when Mr. Conley gave him the chocolate bar, it stuck to his hand. Then Mr. Conley took a cold lemon soda pop from the icebox. He opened the bottle and gave it to Shan. The ice-cold bottle felt good in his hot hand.

"Did your mother send for anything, Shan?" Mr. Con-

Shan turned the bottle up to his mouth.

ley asked. "I see you fetched a basket."

"Yes, sir," he replied. "The list is in the bottom of the basket."

Shan turned the bottle up to his mouth. He was in a big hurry to taste again his favorite drink. He swallowed and tasted and then he looked at the bottle. It was lemon soda pop but it didn't taste like the others he'd got at Mr. Conley's. It wasn't as good as the others had been. Then he took a bite from his chocolate bar. It had a funny taste, too. It didn't taste as good as the other chocolate bars Mr. Conley had sold him. He looked at the wrapper; it was the same kind of chocolate bar he had been getting. He looked around to see where Mr. Conley was. He was reading the list Shan's mother had sent.

Shan took another bite from the chocolate bar. Then he followed it with a cool drink of his soda pop. That's the way he had always done. He'd eaten one and drunk the other and the two were wonderful together. But they weren't so good now. There was something funny about the taste of both. He took another bite of the chocolate bar and another drink of soda pop. He was in a hurry because Mr. Conley had filled the basket and was fetching it to him. Then Mr. Conley might go back to the sacks. He hurried to finish the chocolate bar and he almost choked. But he washed the bite down with another drink of soda pop.

"I have everything your mother wanted, Shan," Mr. Conley said, setting the basket down on the counter.

Shan hated to leave any lemon soda pop in the bottle. He put the bottle to his lips while Mr. Conley stood there

42

watching him. He couldn't swallow the last drink. He choked and the soda pop almost strangled him. He set the bottle on the counter and grabbed his basket and ran from the store. Mr. Conley stood shaking his head as Shan ran out the door and down the steps. The fresh air outside the store was better for Shan. Still, he didn't feel just right as he began running up the valley road for home.

"Did you take that flour sack down to Mr. Conley's store?" . . .

A Penny's Worth of Character

"Shan, what happened to that flour sack with a hole in the bottom?" his mother asked as soon as he reached home.

She stood before him and pointed a finger. There was a frown on her face.

"Answer me, Shan," she said, as she took the basket from his hand.

Shan moved his bare feet restlessly over the stone doorstep. He looked down at his feet, for he couldn't look up at his mother.

"Did you take that flour sack down to Mr. Conley's store?" she asked him again.

"Yes, Mom," he replied.

"I thought I told you not to take it!"

"You did."

"Then why did you do it?"

"I don't know."

"Did Mr. Conley go over the sacks to see if any had

holes in 'em?'' his mother asked.

"Yes, he did," Shan said.

"Why didn't he find the hole in that sack?" she then asked him.

"He didn't look through all of 'em," Shan said.

"You're lucky," she said. "But didn't you know it was wrong to do this? Didn't you know you were cheating Mr. Conley for a penny?"

"Yes, Mom," he said.

"Then why did you do it?"

"I wanted a dime, Mom," he said. "If I had taken nine sacks, I would have had only nine cents. I wanted a chocolate bar and a bottle of lemon soda pop. That took a dime."

"You know I never taught you to do a thing like this, don't you?" his mother said.

And then she didn't say another word. She turned and walked back through the house with the basket. Shan's thoughts spun around and around and over and over in his head for he wondered what his mother was going to do now. He didn't have long to wait to find out what it was. She came back immediately with a new sack.

"Let this be a lesson to you," his mother said. "Take this sack to Mr. Conley to replace the no-good one. Tell him just what has happened."

"Oh no, Mom," he said, "I . . . I . . . can't. . . ."

"You will," she said firmly.

"Won't you just whip me and let me stay here?" he begged, beginning to cry. "I don't want to tell Mr. Conley what I've done."

"Go back and make things right," his mother said. "You will think before you ever do this again."

Shan looked up at his mother and his eyes were filled with tears.

"I want to say one more thing, Mom," he said. "It's just one sack that's only worth a penny."

"One penny or a hundred pennies, Shan, the principle is the same," his mother told him. "Do you remember that story your teacher told you about Abraham Lincoln when he was working in the store? He made a mistake of just a couple of pennies when he was giving a woman her change. Abraham Lincoln walked miles after a hard day's work to return it to her. That's how important it was to him. It made him feel better inside. It will make you feel better, too."

Shan stood before his own front door crying. He didn't want to go back.

"Dry your tears," his mother told him. "Be on your way!"

There wasn't anything for Shan to do but turn and go back to the store, carrying one little light paper sack. The sack was only worth a penny and he had a mile to walk there and back. As he walked down the road with the sack under his arm, he turned and looked back to see what his mother was doing. She was standing at their front door watching him walk slowly under the August sunlight down the hot, dusty road.

. . . the world had belonged to him. But now it was different.

THE ROAD BACK

Earlier in the morning, when Shan had gone to the store with his ten sacks, the world had belonged to him. But now it was different. He walked under a hot sun down the dusty road and this world didn't belong to him. This was a world he didn't want. When he reached the giant sycamore where he had watched the big redheaded woodpecker early that morning boring for worms, he stopped long enough to look up to see if the bird was back again, for it would soon be time for lunch. But the woodpecker had gone and the dead limb looked hot and dry in the August sunlight. He wondered where the woodpecker had gone and if he was in a cool nest in some hollow tree with his family of young birds away from the hot sun.

Beyond the sycamore, he walked over sand that was hot to his feet. The buttercups, over which the honeybees and bumblebees were humming two hours ago, were dry and wilting in the heat.

When Shan reached the big white oak, he wondered if bees and birds sweated as he did. He thought the birds didn't, for when the sun got hot, he never saw many birds—they were always in the cool shade. They gathered food in the morning when it was cool. He looked over the steep bank by the white oak at the deep water hole. The minnows weren't swimming around either. He saw them resting down there in the shaded water. A lazy minnow swam up, expecting Shan to throw a cracker crumb or a green fly, but Shan didn't—he didn't have time. And the minnow wasn't as pretty as it had been that morning when Shan felt the world belonged to him. He'd let the minnows find their own food. He had to work to get his. Look what the chocolate bar and the soda pop had cost him! He wasn't through yet. Look what a time he was having! Besides, his bare feet were hot from walking over the sun-baked sand.

When he waded into the stream he touched a rock with his foot and a crawdad came out swimming backward. Shan didn't stop to watch it swim. He waded under the willow shades where the water was cooler to his feet. But he was careful not to splash water on the good sack he was carrying. He knew he had to give that to Mr. Conley. And he had to tell him about the sack with the hole in it. He dreaded to do that, too. He hoped there wouldn't be any customers to hear him.

When Shan walked over the sand bar, he didn't stop. He walked on and dried the tears from his eyes the best he could with the back of his hand. The turtle that had come to the sand bar to lay her eggs that morning was

Shan thought of running away from home.

somewhere under the cool shade of the alders and the willows beside the stream.

Leaves on the big sugar maple were wilted, too. The hawks were no longer circling in the high blue sky. Shan walked slowly down the dusty road beyond the maple, thinking about Mr. Conley and the sack. He wondered what he would say when he gave it to him. He didn't want to take this sack to Mr. Conley.

Shan thought of running away from home. He thought about taking to the hills and going in any direction that would take him from home. Then he wondered how he could leave his father. His father didn't have any part in making him take the sack back and explain to Mr. Conley why he was bringing it back. And he thought about how hard it would be to stay away from his baby brother and his little sisters. Shan wanted to make his mother feel sorry for sending him back to the store with a sack worth a penny.

But there wasn't anything left for him to do but to face Mr. Conley. To think of returning this sack made his face get hotter than the sun could make it. He tried to think of what he was going to say. But his tongue got heavy again. It was as lazy as the wind and didn't want to speak these words. It would only be a few minutes. He couldn't tell his heart to beat slower and he couldn't keep his face from getting hotter.

He walked around the bend in the road where the cliffs looked up to the hot blue sky. This was the first time in Shan's life he hadn't wanted to see Mr. Conley's little white store under the sycamore trees. Always before, when he had walked around the winding road beneath these cliffs and seen the store, he had started running to get there. He saw two horses, with saddles on, hitched to the sycamore limbs. There was a team of horses hitched to a wagon standing in front of the store. Shan thought, people are in the store and they will hear what I have to tell Mr. Conley. I'll wait until they leave before I give him this sack.

Shan stopped outside and looked in.

MAKING A WRONG RIGHT

Shan stopped outside and looked in. There were three men inside. Tom Eversole picked up his basket of groceries and walked out. Then Shan walked softly inside and listened to Mr. Conley count the eggs Manuel Greene had brought. He watched Manuel Greene trade his eggs for groceries. He stood in the back of the store so quietly they didn't see him. Then Manuel Greene put his basket of groceries on his arm and left the store. Only Tom Crum was left. He asked Mr. Conley for a sack of meal and flour. Mr. Conley picked up the sack on top and filled it full of meal from the barrel. He weighed it to see if he had ten pounds. He had eleven pounds and he slowly dipped a pound out, watching his scales to see that they were correct. Shan watched, too.

Then Mr. Conley got the second sack. He dipped a scoop of flour from the barrel into the sack. Then he dipped another and another as if he were in a hurry. Shan saw the flour stream through the corner of the sack like water pouring through the holes in a sieve.

"Woops," Mr. Conley shouted as he put the sack down on the floor as quickly as he could to save the flour.

"Tom, did I tear that sack?" Mr. Conley said, looking up at Tom Crum.

"Don't think you did," Tom replied.

"I just bought this sack about three hours ago from Shan Shelton," he said. "He brought me ten sacks and I looked at nearly all of 'em to see if there were any holes."

Shan was standing behind Mr. Conley and Tom Crum and they hadn't seen him yet.

"These are the first sacks I've used today," Mr. Conley said. "See what it has cost me because I didn't look inside the other two sacks."

"You can't trust young'uns nowadays," Tom Crum said. "They're not raised right."

"Nope, I don't guess you can," Mr. Conley said. "But I'd miss 'em if they didn't come in here and trade me sacks, roots, herbs, eggs, and pelts for candy and soda pop. I like to have 'em around."

When Mr. Conley had finished saying these words he looked back and saw Shan with an empty sack in his hand. He looked straight at Shan. Tom Crum turned around to look.

"Want something, Shan?" Mr. Conley said.

"Yes," Shan said.

He walked up, his heart beating faster and the sweat running from his face. He gave Mr. Conley the sack.

"Just one?" Mr. Conley said.

Shan saw the flour stream through the corner of the sack . . .

"Yes," Shan said as Mr. Conley opened the sack to look for holes.

"No use to look for a hole," Shan said.

"Oh," he said, then he laughed as he started to open his candy case.

"No candy for that one, Mr. Conley," Shan said.

"Why, what do you mean?" Mr. Conley asked. "Don't you want the penny?"

"I brought it because—" Shan couldn't finish saying what he wanted to tell Mr. Conley. His tongue was heavier than the wilted pods of leaves hanging over the hot road.

"You've got a good mother," Mr. Conley said.

Shan hadn't told Mr. Conley it was his mother who had sent him back with the sack. He wondered how Mr. Conley knew.

He remembered the thoughts he had had about his mother. He remembered thinking of running away from home to make her feel sorry because she had made him bring the good sack to Mr. Conley.

"There'll be a reserved seat in Heaven for your mother," Mr. Conley said as Shan wiped the tears from his eyes with the back of his hand.

"You'll always be thankful when you grow up your mother made you do this, Shan," Tom Crum said as he rubbed his big rough hand over his beardy face. "This is a lesson in honesty you won't forget. It gives you a good foundation from your finger tips to your toes!"

"Mr. Conley, I'll bring you more sacks to pay for the flour you lost." Shan sobbed and turned to leave the store.

"Since you've been so honest, Shan," Mr. Conley said, smiling, "your debt is paid. I didn't lose much flour. And I think more of you than I have ever thought in my life."

Shan ran from the store. Mr. Conley said something to Tom Crum. Shan didn't hear what he said. He didn't want to hear, for it didn't matter now. The warm lazy wind felt so good to his face. The air was as good and fresh to breathe as it had been when the dew was on the buttercups. The lazy wind dried the flow of tears that had come to his eyes in the store. These were tears he had tried to hold back.

Shan felt as light as a June bug in the August wind. He knew now how Abraham Lincoln felt after he had returned the pennies. Something had left him, and he started running up the valley road for home. The blue sky above him was as beautiful as he had ever seen it. A redbird chirruped lazily from a cluster of pawpaw and its chirruping was more beautiful than its spring song before an April shower. A hawk sailed over in the lazy wind and it was pretty, too. Shan didn't fear anything now. His mother had been right when she said he would feel better within. How did she know all these things? He knew now that his mother was smart and good.

The turtle was back on the sand bar and Shan ran up to her. She put her head back and went into her shell. "She's done that so I can pet her!" Shan shouted to the wind. "She knows I've heard that once she bit a person she wouldn't let loose until it thundered or the sun went

He knew now that his mother was smart and good.

down!" Shan gently stroked her hard back.

Then he ran on because it was past his lunchtime. He could tell by the sun, for he could step on the head of his shadow. He was hungry, too. He ran into the water again, splashing it in all directions as the big feet of one of his father's horses did. The beautiful crawdads must have thought he was a horse for they came from under their little rock houses. They swam backward in all directions. They were beautiful again to Shan as they pulled the water with their fan-shaped tails. In the cool waters under the alder and willow shades, the minnows swam like arrows of flying silver.

Shan looked down and saw himself in the mirror of sky-blue water and he was smiling. No one could tell by looking at his eyes now that he had ever cried. He had never been so happy. And the whole world was happy because he was. His world had never been so beautiful before and it belonged to him again.

"Hello, Mom," he called to his mother as he came near the house. "I'm home."

ABOUT THE AUTHOR

Jesse Stuart (1906-1984) was one of America's best-known and best-loved writers. During his lifetime he published more than 2,000 poems and 460 short stories, and, in addition, he produced more than 30 works of fiction, biography, and autobiography—over 60 published volumes—which have immortalized his native hill country.

Jesse Stuart also taught and lectured extensively. His teaching experience ranged from the one-room schoolhouses of his youth in eastern Kentucky to the American University in Cairo, Egypt, and embraced years of service as school superintendent, high school teacher, and high school principal. "First, last, always," said Jesse Stuart, "I am a teacher . . . Good teaching is forever, and the teacher is immortal."

ABOUT THE ILLUSTRATOR

Rocky Zornes is an accomplished graphic artist with a unique talent for book design and illustration, and a special sensitivity to Jesse Stuart's eastern Kentucky homeland. He is a graduate of Paul Blazer High School in Ashland, and later earned his B.A. and M.A. degrees in art from Morehead State University. He owns and operates ZAK Productions in Lexington, Kentucky.

Jesse Stuart's Illustrated Junior Books

Andy Finds a Way, $6 softback, $12 hardback
The Beatinest Boy, $5 softback
Bluetick Pig, $10 softback, $20 hardback
Come to My Tomorrowland, $10 softback, $17.50 hardback
Old Ben, $4 softback, $10 hardback
A Penny's Worth of Character, $5 softback
Red Mule, $6 softback
A Ride With Huey the Engineer, $6 softback
The Rightful Owner, $6 softback, $12 hardback

Set Discount
Save $23. A softback set of Jesse Stuart's nine illustrated
Junior Books, especially designed for readers in grades 3-7,
regularly sells for $58. Order today and get this set of nine
books for only $35.

School Discount
While supplies last, the JSF offers classroom sets of 30 or
more books at a 40% discount.

Study Guide
Winners is a unique study guide for Stuart's Junior Books.
The stories and the language arts activities will encourage
pride in the children's culture and in themselves.
The self-concept activities will reinforce both their view of
personal worth and traditional American values. The 141-page
workbook comes in a three-ring binder for ease in copying
worksheets. Only $27.50.

Jesse Stuart Foundation
P. O. Box 669 • Ashland, KY 41105-0669
606-326-1667 • FAX 606-325-2519
e-mail jsf@jsfbooks.com
www.jsfbooks.com